I AM THE STORM

For Karl, storm fighter.
—JY

For Jamie, who has weathered all storms with grace.
And for Nathan and Alex by her side,
strong and powerful.
—HEYS

To Margo, our little force of nature.
—KH & KH

RISE x Penguin Workshop
An Imprint of Penguin Random House LLC, New York

Text copyright © 2020 by Jane Yolen and Heidi E. Y. Stemple. Illustrations copyright © 2020 by Kristen and Kevin Howdeshell. All rights reserved. Published by Rise × Penguin Workshop, an imprint of Penguin Random House LLC, New York. PENGUIN and PENGUIN WORKSHOP are trademarks of Penguin Books Ltd. The W colophon is a registered trademark and the RISE colophon is a trademark of Penguin Random House LLC. Manufactured in China.

The text is set in Hand Scribble Sketch Times.
The art is sketched in pencil and the finishes are rendered in Photoshop with a Wacom tablet.
Edited by Cecily Kaiser
Designed by Maria Elias

Visit us online at www.penguinrandomhouse.com.

Library of Congress Cataloging-in-Publication Data is available upon request.

ISBN 9780593222751   10 9 8 7 6 5 4 3 2 1

I AM THE STORM

by Jane Yolen and Heidi E. Y. Stemple

illustrated by Kristen and Kevin Howdeshell

RISE

NEW YORK

When the wind howled and blew,
loud as a train,

we had a party in the basement with Grandma,
reading books and playing games with the flashlight.

When the wind stopped whirling,
as tornadoes always do,
we picked up branches and fixed the fence.
I danced round and round our front yard,
howling and blowing like the wind.

When the ice and snow fell,
sparkling like fairy dust on the windows,
and all the lights went out,
we made a fire
and cooked hot dogs and marshmallows.

When the ice and snow stopped falling,
as blizzards always do,
we shoveled our walk and Mrs. Garcia's, too.

We built a snowman, and I tossed up big
handfuls of snow that fell down on my head.

When the fires burned in a forest nearby,
Papa drove us to the lake.
We camped out and made new friends.
I picked wildflowers and tied them into bouquets.

When the forests cooled,
as wildfires always do,
I brought flowers to all the neighbors
while the grown-ups swept the ashes
and washed windows.

The air still felt hot as I swayed
with my arms up, like a slow beautiful flame.
We had big bowls of ice cream to cool down.

When the sea swirled and roiled and rose,
almost into the sky,

we drove away from the ocean
to my cousins' house.
We pretended the bunk beds were boats,
high above the waves.

The storm was strong,
and I was scared.

But when the wind
and sea calmed,
as hurricanes always do,
we went back home.

It's okay to be scared.

Nature is strong and powerful.
But, I am strong and powerful, too.

I am wild
like the blizzard.

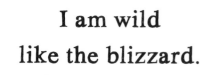

I am loud
like the tornado.

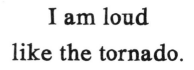

I am hot
like the fire.

I am fierce
like the hurricane.

I am the storm.

And when the storm passes,
as it always does,
I am the calm, too.